# Ace's Basement

## Ted Staunton

*Orca currents*

WITHDRAWN

ORCA BOOK PUBLISHERS

**Library and Archives Canada Cataloguing in Publication**

Staunton, Ted, 1956-
Ace's basement / Ted Staunton.
(Orca currents)

Issued also in electronic format.
ISBN 978-1-4598-0438-8 (bound).--ISBN 978-1-4598-0437-1 (pbk.)

I. Title.  II. Series: Orca currents
PS8587.T334A34 2013      jc813'.54      C2013-901919-7

First published in the United States, 2013
**Library of Congress Control Number:** 2013935379

**Summary:** Ace learns about Internet bullying while trying
to get a music career off the ground.

*Orca Book Publishers is dedicated to preserving the environment and has
printed this book on Forest Stewardship Council® certified paper.*

Orca Book Publishers gratefully acknowledges the support for its
publishing programs provided by the following agencies: the Government
of Canada through the Canada Book Fund and the Canada Council for the Arts,
and the Province of British Columbia through the BC Arts Council
and the Book Publishing Tax Credit.

Cover photography by iStockphoto.com

ORCA BOOK PUBLISHERS
PO Box 5626, Stn. B
Victoria, BC Canada
V8R 6S4

ORCA BOOK PUBLISHERS
PO Box 468
Custer, WA USA
98240-0468

www.orcabook.com
Printed and bound in Canada.

16 15 14 13 • 4 3 2 1

*My thanks to Will and Union Duke for great music and technical info, and to Melanie Jeffs for super editing and YouTube know-how. You're all aces with me.*

# Chapter One

Lisa is playing acoustic guitar and singing.

*What's up? I'm down*
*When you're not around...*

It's Friday after school. We're busking for change in front of the liquor store. I'm on acoustic guitar and harmonica.

I have the harmonica on one of those holders that loops around your neck. The guy at the music store called it a harp rack because harmonicas are also called mouth harps. It looks like the world's biggest dental retainer. Usually I play bass, but when we play outside, there's no place to plug in my amp.

Lisa sways as she sings. It's nice to watch, especially if you stand behind her like I do. Not only does Lisa have a killer voice, she's also hot. These are two big reasons why the open guitar case between us has money in it. Another reason is we sound good—as long as I don't sing. Our duo is named Two. Our sound is sort of folky, but not too mellow. I keep the rhythm going. Lisa sings.

*I could trip, I could fall*
*Would you hear if I called...*

I wrote that. I'm getting better at lyrics. Lisa and I write songs together a lot. When you're only in grade nine and ten, there are not a lot of places to play, so we busk and we get together and write. Life could be worse. Sitting knee to knee with Lisa and making up songs is not a bad way to pass the time. She always has ideas. She has great knees too.

*Over and over and over and over*
*Coming apart at the dreams...*

Lisa's voice goes high. The liquor store is busy. Friday afternoon is a good time to busk here. People leaving the store toss coins in the case. I have time to call "Thanks!" before I close my eyes for my big harmonica solo.

Harmonica is new for me. My guess is that playing it is a lot like heavy kissing. You have to time your breathing in and out and move your tongue around and stuff—not to get too gross about it. Plus you have to know where to start. I haven't figured that out with kissing. There's no one for me to practice with.

I have practiced harmonica though. My solo starts with blowing out on the fourth hole. I blow. The wrong note comes out. The next note is wrong too. And the next one and the next. *What is going on?* I have to keep playing, but it's panic time.

This is a nightmare. It's as if everything is backward. That's when it hits me that everything *is* backward. I have cleverly put the harp upside down in the rack. Oh. No.

Just as I figure this out, the harp starts slipping away like an elevator going down. The stupid wing nuts that hold the rack have come loose again. *Aargh.* I chase the harmonica down my chest, playing more horrible noise. Maybe I can pretend this is jazz.

I keep my eyes shut. Maybe people will pity me if they think I'm blind.

I hear Lisa saying "What are you—" I can't answer. I'm bent double as I squish out the last awful sound. I open my eyes.

There's a cell phone right in my face. "AAAAH!" I jump. The harp rack flies up and bonks my forehead. I yell again and grab my head. The harmonica pops out, bounces off my guitar and into the guitar case. I stagger into it too. *Crunch*. Change goes flying.

"All *right*!"

"Trash it!"

"Rock out!"

Three beefy guys with six-packs of beer and the I-need-a-shave look are cheering. They throw coins into the case. Some of them bounce off my foot.

"You should be on *Saturday Night Live*," one calls as they walk away. I don't think he means as a musical guest.

"Ace, are you okay?" Lisa asks. "What happened?"

I'm still rubbing my forehead. I don't dare look at her yet. Instead, I glare at the owner of the cell phone that was just in my face. It's my friend Denny. I should have known.

"That was *so* cool," Denny says, looking at the screen on his phone.

"Thanks a whole bunch, Den."

"No sweat," he says. Denny is not good at understanding when other people are being sarcastic, especially me. He waves his phone at us. "You know what you two need? A YouTube video."

## Chapter Two

Lisa's dad picks her up when we're done. He nods and says, "Hi, David" to me. David is my real name. Ace is my nickname. He says hi to Denny, too, which is more than Lisa has said to Denny since he showed up. I get the feeling Lisa doesn't like Denny that much. Right now I'm a little bugged with him myself for freaking me out with his cell phone. It's almost as if the whole harmonica mess was his fault.

Lisa and I split the money we made. There is a little more than eighteen dollars each. It's not our best for a Friday, but it's good. *We* were good, apart from my harmonica disaster.

"Practice tomorrow?" I ask her.

"Can't," she says. "I'm working all day." She has a part-time job at Bargain Village. Sometimes I drop by there when she's working and pretend I didn't know she would be there.

"How about Sunday?" I ask. "Maybe?"

Lisa makes a face. "I have an English report. Haven't you got homework?"

"Yeah," I say. I do have homework. Whether I do it is another thing. That's how I got my nickname. When people used to ask what marks I had gotten, I'd always say sarcastically, "A's," even though they weren't.

Lisa waves and follows her dad to their car. She has her phone out, texting, before she even gets in. She's still texting as they pull away. I wave anyway. Then I start walking home with Denny. We take a shortcut through the park.

He shows me what he filmed. Let's just say it's not pleasing.

"Wow, Den," I say, "the close-up where my eyes bug out while I scream is really tasteful. How can I thank you?"

"Hey, no biggie," Denny says. He still doesn't get that I'm being sarcastic. Instead, he blathers more about doing a video. Denny is big on video. He's in the video club at school. There are hot girls in the video club.

As we pass the swings, I have a conversation in my head instead of listening to him. First I say, *Why didn't you ask Lisa if she's busy tonight, dumb one?* I answer, *She was texting. That means she's busy. And I didn't want to interrupt. And her dad was in a hurry.* Then I say to myself, *You're chicken. That's the real reason.* That makes me answer, *Okay, just watch. I'll text her when I get home.* That makes me feel better—if I don't think about how many times I've said that before and then not sent the text.

At the other side of the park, Denny takes off for his house. It's close to suppertime when I get home, but I still get back before Mom. She sells real estate, so her schedule is weird sometimes. The sound of hammering from the basement tells me that her boyfriend, Chuck, is here though. Chuck sells real estate too. He's renovating our basement in his spare time. I thought it was fine the way it was. He says he's making a man cave for me down there. Uh-huh.

Our cat, Archie, comes to say hello. I check Arch's food and water, then look downstairs. Chuck is on his hands and knees, measuring something.

He's flashing some major plumber's butt. It's not a pretty sight.

"That you, Dave?" he calls up, still measuring.

"Uh-huh."

"How was busking?"

"Okay." I'm not going to tell him about the harmonica. Chuck is actually an okay guy. He was in a band when he first dated my mom. It's his guitar and bass I've been using. I'm not going to tell him about stepping in the guitar case either, since the case is his too. Luckily, it only cracked a little. Instead I say, "Denny says we need a video."

"Hmm. Good idea," Chuck says. He marks a two-by-four with a pencil, sticks the pencil behind his ear and stands up. It's a better visual, believe me. Then he chuckles and says, "Or maybe not. When I was in Razorburn, we tried to make a video. Remind me to tell you about it sometime."

Razorburn was Chuck's band. They played country rock. He stoops and grabs the two-by-four. I get to enjoy more plumber's butt. Then he moves to his portable workbench and picks up the circular saw.

That's when my mom gets home. She has pizza with her. She gets me to help make salad, and then, as we all eat, Chuck tells her about Denny's video idea. Naturally, she has a million suggestions. All of them are bad.

"You know what you could do," she says, "is have you and Lisa both singing, with your heads in profile next to one another, like, you know—oh, whose video was it?"

"ABBA," I say. It's one of my favorite bad videos to laugh at.

"Right." Mom is all excited. "And you could—"

Oh, please. I nod and pretend I'm listening. Really, I'm talking to myself again. *Text Lisa.* I chew slower and answer: *Grade-ten girls don't hang with grade-nine guys, even if they do play music together.* I know this is a law of the universe—or of high school, at least. High school and the universe are the same thing if you are fourteen.

*It doesn't have to be a law,* I say to myself. *Didn't you hear how worried she sounded when she asked if you were all right? Do it. Don't be a chicken.*

I'm going to do it. I put down my pizza and pull out my phone. Mom says, "Hey, mister, no phones at the table, remember?" At that exact instant, her BlackBerry rings and she jumps up. "Except for this one call," Mom says.

Chuck takes salad. I power my phone to text Lisa. The pizza has gone dry in my mouth. I'm going to do it. I'm going to text her this time. But first I see a message from Denny: **want 2c doomaster 2nite can pick u up @ 8.**

13

Oh, wow. *Doom Master*. It's a new 3-D blockbuster movie. It's based on our favorite action-hero toy from when Denny and I were little. This is opening night, so everybody will be going. Lisa will probably even be there. That would solve everything. I text Denny back: **cool c u @ 8.**

I can always ask Lisa next time.

# Chapter Three

Lisa isn't at the movie. When I acciden-
tally-on-purpose go by Bargain Village
on Saturday, she's on a break. I don't
see her till lunch on Monday, when
we meet in the music room at school.
The music teacher lets us use the
school's equipment to mix our recording
of "Coming Apart at the Dreams." It's a

good thing Lisa takes music. Next year I will, for sure.

"*I could trip, I could—*" Lisa clicks the computer mouse at two minutes and thirty-seven seconds. We're at the repeat of the first verse. The whole song is only three minutes and twelve seconds.

"Right there," she says. "My voice sounds so lame there."

"No, it doesn't," I say. "We've talked about this before, Lee."

Lisa's family calls her Lee. After she phoned me one time and said, "Hi, it's Lee," I figured it was cool if I used it too. I still get a little nervous when I do though.

"But I'm flat," Lisa complains.

"No, you're not. We checked, remember? It just needs to sound stronger."

"Maybe we should double the vocal," Lisa says.

"You're going to sing it again?"

"No, no. With this program I can copy the vocal to another track and play them both. Wait."

She starts pointing and clicking the mouse again. Screens blink past us. *How cool is this?* I think. I'm sitting here mixing a song that I cowrote with Lisa, who I get to call Lee. And she is older than me and gorgeous and in a duo called Two with me, and I'm talking and not nervous or sarcastic. I didn't even think of a smart comment when Lisa said she was flat. I bet you thought I would, too. So, if I'm comfortable with her when we work on music, how come I can't ask her to a movie?

"Okay, let's try this." Lisa clicks the mouse one more time.

*I could trip, I could fall*
*Would you hear if I called...*

Lisa's voice sounds way fuller. "Awesome," I say. "That is so cool, Lee. How'd you do that?"

Before she can show me, guess who barges in?

"Ace! Lee! Hey, wait'll you hear this." Yes. It's Denny.

I glare at him. I'm the one who gets to call Lisa Lee. And anyway, what does he want now? I say, "No, Den, wait'll you hear *this*." I reach for the mouse to click on a playback. I knock over my carton of chocolate milk instead. It splashes onto my backpack. I jump up "Aw—"

"No, listen," Denny insists. "We want to do a YouTube video, right?"

"*You* want to do a YouTube video. We didn't say we did." While I talk, I use my gym shorts to mop up the milk. I know this is probably a mistake even while I'm doing it.

"Whatever," Denny says. "So anyway, I told Nadia and Alison *Ace needs a YouTube music video* and they were, like, *We're on it!*"

"Yeah right," I say. I'm still mopping up. Now I see the milk has gone *into* my backpack. "And it's not *my* video, it's Two's—"

"Nadia and Alison who?" Lisa interrupts. At least she's talking to Denny today.

"You know," Denny says. "From video club."

Lisa doesn't say anything. I'm too busy mopping the inside of my backpack to look at her. I've known Alison and Nadia since they were in a grade one/two class with me and Denny. We were grade ones. They were grade twos. They've gotten a lot hotter since then, but I know they don't think we have.

Before I can say, "Yeah right" again, Nadia and Alison come in.

"Sweet," Denny says. "So, let's make a cool music video and conquer YouTube!"

I lift up my chocolate-milk-covered shorts. The room goes quiet. I look at the shorts. Oh-oh. Using them *was* a mistake. I stuff them in my pack.

But now I see no one is looking at me. Lisa is looking at Nadia and Alison, and they are looking at her. If looks could kill, they'd all be six feet under.

Nadia says, "Actually, Denny, maybe not. So much to do, you know. Sorry, Ace. Too bad, so sad. Gotta go."

"So *not* sad, Lisa," says Alison. "We're outta here."

They spin on their heels. Alison tugs up a shoulder strap. Nadia pulls the hem of her shirt down to the top of her jeans. Is that a tattoo peeking out there? They walk out. A second later, from down the hall, a girl's voice calls, "Oh, Robb*yyyyyyyyy,*" then there's laughter.

"What was that about?" Denny scrunches up his nose.

"We're not exactly friends," Lisa says. Her face is as red as her hair.

"How come?" Denny asks. He's not Mister Sensitive. I glare at him. But I want to know too.

"It's a long boring story," Lisa says. "About boys."

Boys? I don't think I want to hear anything about Lisa and boys.

"Okay, whatever," Denny says. "Anyway, we don't need them to do our video. They were just gonna help with tech stuff anyway. Really, it's my vision—well, *our* vision, right, Lee?"

"Right," I join in, "because *I* don't have any vision."

"Well, like, you too, Ace. But it will feature Lee, right? I mean, she's the lead singer." Denny isn't even looking at me while he talks. He's looking at Lisa. And calling her Lee.

"I don't know," Lisa says.

"Come on," Denny urges. "It'll be way cooler than busking. It's creative! People will hear your songs. And I've already tweeted that we're doing it."

It's time for Denny to go. I pull out my chocolate-milk gym shorts and wave them in his face. "We'll think about it, Den. It's time for gym. Go get your stuff."

"Whoa." He waves his hands. "If it's wrestling again today, we are so not partners."

Denny leaves. Lisa and I play "Coming Apart at the Dreams" again. People *should* hear this song. Denny is probably useless at videos, but you never know. And it would mean I'd get to spend more time with Lisa, even if it was with Denny around. At least I could keep an eye on him.

Lisa shuts down the computer. The bell is ringing. We look at each other.

"Let's do it," I say. "We don't want to busk forever, right? What have we got to lose? If it sucks, we don't post it and nobody sees." Lisa doesn't say anything.

I have a brain wave. "And if it works," I say, "Nadia and Alison are going to be really jealous."

Lisa starts to smile, then bites her lip. Outside, the hall is getting noisy.

Finally she nods. "Okay," she says. "But *we* say if it's good or bad. Oh no, I'm gonna be late." She grabs her stuff and heads out, texting like mad. "Later," she calls.

I grab my stuff too. The chocolate milk has made everything sticky. Wow, I think, that was easy. So why can't I ask her to a movie?

## Chapter Four

Amazingly, my chocolate-milk shorts have gotten me excused from gym class. This is great, because I hate wrestling. Guys my size get turned into pretzels. Instead, I get to untangle and refold all the volleyball nets in the equipment room.

After school I tell Denny, "We're gonna go for it."

"Sick," Denny says. He tweets the news to the world as we walk to my house. "We should talk over shots for the video. I've got a notebook. You write them down." He unzips his backpack. Then he says, "Hey, look. I almost forgot." He pulls out a shiny action figure.

"Doom Master!" I laugh. "Where'd you find it?" When we were little kids, we both had Doom Master toys. Everybody did. We'd have action-figure wars with them.

"In my basement," Denny says, "after we saw the movie. I thought my mom had thrown it out."

I take the toy from Denny. I hook its mechanical claws to the lip of a litter bin. "Doom Master escapes!" I say. Denny whips out his cell phone and takes a picture. "What else can we pose him with?" he says.

"I know," I say. "C'mon. I'll show you at my place." The video can wait. This is too good.

When we had our old band, Denny and I practiced in my basement a lot. Denny hasn't been over as much since he started with video club. This is Denny's first look at the man cave Chuck is working on. "Cool," he says when we get downstairs. "I think. Is he going to fill in the wall around the washroom?"

"Well, yeah, Den. He'll probably even hook up the toilet too. But look at this."

Chuck's power tools are lying around. I pose Doom Master by the electric drill. With the drill bit pointing out, it looks like he's battling a giant death ray or something.

"Awesome." Denny takes the picture. We put Doom Master on the circular saw and in the jaws of a monkey wrench. We pose him holding a screwdriver as big as he is. "I wish there was more zoom on this camera," Denny says. "I should come back with my mom's."

Archie the cat comes down to join us. Arch is not interested in taking Doom Master for a ride on his back. I think I've had enough of Doom Master too.

"So let's think about the video, Den," I say. I dig out my notebook and pen. They smell like chocolate milk, and the book is a little soggy. Maybe I should wash out my backpack.

Denny is busy. He's got Doom Master clutching a guitar string that was lying around. He's hung the string from a nail on one of the two-by-fours framing the bathroom wall. He swings Doom Master back and forth. Now Arch is interested. He bats at Doom Master with a paw. Denny takes more pictures.

"Den," I say. "The video?"

"Yeah. Okay. In a sec." He takes a few more pictures. Then we flop into the two beanbag chairs, the only furniture down here right now.

"So," I say, "it starts '*What's up? I'm down / When you're not around...*'"

Denny says, "For that, let's have you two singing on a roof. No, wait! You playing guitar on a roof, Lee singing down below on the street, like."

"It better be a flat roof," I say. "I'm scared of heights."

"We could tie you to a chimney or something."

I like that it would look as if Lisa was singing to me, but I don't say that. I write *roof* on the last page of my notebook. It's got a faint brown stain across the bottom. Oh well, if we get famous, we can probably auction this page off for a million dollars. Stains and wrinkles will make it cooler.

"Okay, next words," I say. "*I could trip, I could fall / Would you hear if I called?*"

"Easy," Denny laughs. "That's my shot of you messing up while you're busking."

"Dream on, Den. No way."

"Just kidding," Denny says. "What if we had a cell phone falling into a toilet?"

We can't agree on whose phone to waste, so that idea is a no-go.

"I know," says Den. "A shot of Lisa singing, and then she dissolves!"

"Yeah, like she shatters into a million pieces—"

"In slow motion!"

"Yeah, in slow motion," I say, writing it down.

"Hey," Denny says, "know how we could do it? If we filmed Lisa looking in that big mirror in your front hall.

We'd have to break it though. Do you think your mom would let us?"

"Hmm. Maybe. She's always saying it makes her look fat. We'll ask when she gets home." I write *mirror* in my notebook too. I'm getting kind of excited. This video could be even more original and creative than songwriting. I mean, I know other people have used these ideas once or twice—okay, a few times more than that—but probably not all together, the way we're going to. That will make it special.

I look up from my notebook. Denny has left his beanbag chair and is posing Doom Master again. There's this silvery hose coming out of the bathroom wall behind the new sink. It's drooping, not hooked up to the sink yet. Denny is trying to hook Doom Master's feet under the handle near the end of the hose. He gives the handle a twist.

Water blasts across the man cave. Denny yells and jumps away.

"At least it's not chocolate milk," he says when we finally get it turned off. By the time we finish mopping up, I've gotten a text from Lisa: **got sat off 2 shoot cu @ lunch w/ideas.**

## Chapter Five

I get to the music room for lunch before Lisa does. Other kids are here today, but they don't seem to mind if you hang out. Maybe that's why Lisa likes to meet here.

"Can't stay," Lisa says when she hurries in, texting. "I forgot I have a math test next period. I have to study. Walk to my locker with me?"

"Sure," I say. I'm good with being seen with Lisa anytime.

We walk. I hope she doesn't notice the sour-milk smell coming from my backpack. I really have to wash it. I tell her the video ideas Denny and I thought up.

Lisa frowns. She looks even hotter than normal when she frowns. Then she says, "I think Denny should just film us playing the song."

"Playing the song? That's it?" I'm stunned.

"I'd rather do simple and good than tricky and sloppy. And it's not like those are new ideas. We've all seen that stuff a million times."

"Yeah, but it's how we'd put them together."

"Ace, this is Denny we're talking about."

Lisa has a point. Besides, I don't want to be tied to a chimney, and my

33

mom's already said we can't smash her mirror. We turn into the hall where Lisa's locker is.

"Okay," I say. "Where should we film?"

"We'll busk," she says.

I freeze, remembering how I goofed up last Friday. Lisa keeps moving. "Come on," she says, looking around and not at me. "It'll be okay."

I should say, *You're right, you make everything okay* or something like that. Before I can even try for it, we're at Lisa's locker. Now she looks at me. "Tell Denny, okay? Noon Saturday in front of the liquor store."

I nod. Then, as she's about to turn away, I get bumped from behind, and I stumble into her. She grabs me before we both get squished into the lockers.

Behind me, a girl's voice calls, "Nice pic. What a happy couple. Who should we send it to?"

*"IIIIIIII knowwwwwwww,"* says a different girl's voice. I get myself turned around in time to see Nadia and Alison twitching their butts as they hurry off down the hall.

Lisa swears. She starts texting again. I back away. I don't think she even hears my "See you Saturday."

What was *that* all about?

## Chapter Six

I tell Denny Lisa's plan. Denny says he'll tweet up a flash mob for an audience at the liquor store.

Why am I not surprised when no one but Denny shows up? "They're just late," he says. "Flash mobs always are."

Lisa rolls her eyes. I don't even try to be sarcastic. I'm nervous. Maybe it's good that no one is here.

"Cool clothes," Lisa says to me as she takes her guitar out of its case. I've got on my best torn jeans, my black Hendrix T-shirt and a straw porkpie hat. I bought the hat last summer, but I never wear it. You don't want people thinking that you're trying to be cool. Besides, my mom said it looked cute.

I don't say that to Lisa. What I do say is, "Back at you," because Lisa looks fantastic. She's wearing skinny black jeans. She's changed her hair around, and I think she's wearing makeup, because her eyes look darker somehow. But what really knocks me out is her top. It's clingy and hot pink and low-cut, and it's either super tight or Lisa has, um, grown overnight. Whatever. Like I said, she looks fantastic. She slings her guitar strap over her shoulder and starts tuning.

I put on my guitar. It covers Jimi on my T-shirt. Oh well, it's not *my* top everyone is going to be watching. I take off my hat and put on my harp rack. It pretty much blocks my face from my nose down. Oh well, it's not *my* face everyone is going to watch either. And it hides the three zits on my chin.

"Wait," Denny says as I reach for my harmonica box. "Use this instead." He hands me a tiny kid-size harmonica. It's so small, it's like a toy. You could practically fit it up your nose.

"See," Denny says, "I've been thinking." He goes back to posing Doom Master in the guitar case.

"Thinking what?" I say. I try the harmonica. "This doesn't even play all the notes I need. It's stupid."

"Don't you get it?" Denny says. "This way we see you better. You don't have to really play it. I'll just overdub the sound later, from your recording."

Lisa strums a chord and says, "I guess that explains why there's no sound equipment."

"Right." Denny grins. "Sweet, huh? And way easier. It doesn't even matter if you really play."

"So we just stand here on the street corner and *pretend*? Gee, Den, there's a great way to draw a crowd. We won't feel stupid." I'm so bugged that for a second, I forget Denny doesn't get sarcasm.

Lisa just says, "But we have to play in sync with the recording or it won't work."

"Hey!" Denny spreads his arms. "I told you, Lee, I've been thinking. That's why I brought along a boom box"—Denny starts looking around— "with the song loaded"—he's looking some more—"on a USB." Denny stops and scratches his head. If there's a boom box around, it's invisible. "At least, I think I did. I was going to. Maybe I didn't."

"Oh, *super*," I say. By this time, I don't care if Denny gets sarcasm or not. "What do we do now?"

"I have it on my phone," Lisa says. "Maybe we could share the earbuds."

I put the little harmonica in the rack—right side up, not that it matters. It's kind of wobbly in there. Not that *that* matters either. Then I lean in for an earbud. The cord is too short. My guitar bumps Lisa's, and my fretting hand ends up way too close to where she's gotten bigger.

We try filming with Lisa using the earbuds and playing along to the recording while I try to follow her. It doesn't work so great, so we switch and she tries to follow me.

That doesn't work so great either. We're always a bit off. Denny films us anyway as we play the song twice more. We all know it's no good. Plus, I feel dumb pretending to play the mini harmonica, and I feel silly wearing my hat. The few people that walk past stare at us. The only good thing is that I don't fall into the guitar case.

"This isn't working," Lisa says finally.

Denny has taken time out to film Doom Master on a parking meter. "It'll be better with the flash mob," he says. "What time is it?"

"Face it, Den," I say. "No one's coming, and this sucks. What'll we do instead?"

We go to the park. Denny films us on the swings. I wear the earbuds and play guitar while Lisa sings. Did you know it's hard to swing on a swing and play guitar at the same time? Especially if you're trying to keep the swing chains from scratching the guitar? And that swinging makes earbuds pop out? And that it is not easier if a hot girl wearing a tight pink top keeps swinging past?

While I'm learning all of this, I'm getting seasick from the swinging. Denny films us on the slide. He films us leaning against a lamppost. He films us running across the grass. "I still wish there was something we could smash," he says. There isn't. "What if Ace stands on top of the climber and plays?" he suggests.

"No," I say.

"Come on," says Denny. "You were going to stand on a roof, remember?"

"That was different," I say. I'm not going to tell him there was no way I would have actually stood on a roof. I think fast. "This might wreck the guitar." Which reminds me of the scratches I've already put in it. Maybe they're not *that* bad.

We settle for me standing on top of a picnic table. It's not exactly an exciting shot.

"Hey," Denny says, "from this angle I can see up your nose."

"Let's try the merry-go-round," I say.

We have to wait until some little kids get off. Denny passes the time filming Doom Master on the climber. The little kids see it and run over.

"What are you all doing?" asks one of their parents. He's a big guy, and I can't tell if he's suspicious of us or if he thinks we're funny.

Denny babbles away about our video and plays some of it back for the guy. I don't go over to look. I watch the guy instead. From the way he bites his bottom lip to keep from grinning, I'd say he thinks we're funny. I guess this is better than him thinking we're suspicious, but not much.

Denny says, "It's just raw footage. Like, there's no soundtrack yet, and I'm going to overexpose some of it and do some slo-mo, you know?"

Now the guy *definitely* thinks we're funny. His eyebrows go up, and his shoulders start jiggling. Oh, great.

"Let's go to the teeter-totter," I say.

Anywhere is better than here, I'm thinking.

Call it my bad.

# Chapter Seven

At the teeter-totter Denny says, "Let's get some shots of Ace on harmonica."

I'm glad to put the guitar down. When I take out the harmonica box, though, it's not there. Maybe it's on vacation with the boom box Denny forgot.

"I can't play this little one in the rack," I say. "It slips around."

"Then just hold it in your fingers," Denny says. "I'm overdubbing anyway, remember?"

Lisa and I sit on opposite ends of the teeter-totter. It's a pretty good balance. I'm not very big. I hold the little harmonica with one hand and try to play it as we bounce up and down. Denny films us. I've still got the earbuds in, so I try to keep us bouncing in time to the music. The thing is, Lisa's top bounces in time to the music too—a lot. Right in front of my eyes. I have to close them to keep from staring.

"Look happy!" Denny calls.

I open my eyes. How can I look happy? I feel like a dork. Then I see he might not be yelling at me. Lisa definitely does not look happy.

"Stop," she says. "Stop!" She's flapping one hand. Something white is poking out of that low front on her top. It doesn't fit the way it did before.

Then, as her end of the teeter-totter goes down, Lisa hops off—while I'm in the air. I slam down butt first and fall back into the dirt. The earbuds pop out, and the harmonica pops into my mouth.

"Hey!" I squawk, except that what comes out is a sound like an accordion in a fish tank. I'm too stunned to move. I start to struggle up, trying to spit out the stupid harmonica.

Someone grabs me around the waist from behind, hauls me up and Heimlichs me. The harmonica pops out with a soggy gurgle, and I almost blow a few chunks along with it.

"Ho-ly!" Denny says.

The arms around me let go. "Are you okay?" Lisa pants behind me.

"I—Yeah, I think so…" I rub the skin under my rib cage, and I turn to Lisa. She's red in the face and all messed up. The white thing is poking from her neckline again, and another one is about

47

to fall out where the bottom of her top has come away from her jeans.

I guess she sees me noticing this, because her face gets even redder, and she spins away. Then she hurries over to her guitar case, stuffs something inside and snaps the fasteners.

"I have to go now," she says without turning around.

"We've probably got lots anyway," Denny says.

"We do?" I say. I'm still a little shaky. Plus, my butt hurts, and something is choking my neck.

"Sure," says Denny. "We only need, like, three minutes and whatever."

"Okay," Lisa says. "Sorry. Gotta go, there's stuff I have to do. Sorry. I forgot. I'll text you or something, Ace."

"Yeah, okay." I'm guessing this isn't a good time to ask if she's busy tonight. Then I remember. "Hey, I've got your phone." I limp over, unwinding the earbud wire from my neck. That's what was choking me.

"Thanks." Lisa takes the phone from me. She's still red in the face. I'm trying not to look at her deflated top. "Later," she says and heads out of the park, texting.

"Wow, how cool was that?" Denny says when I limp back to him. "She popped her chicken cutlets."

"Den," I say, "shut up."

# Chapter Eight

Denny says he's going to go home and start editing.

"There's nothing worth editing," I say as I snap my guitar case shut and pick up my hat.

"Hey," Denny says. "Leave it to the, uh, magician and his apprentices."

"*Sorcerer* and his apprentices," I say. If Denny has apprentices, I'm Santa Claus—and the world is in big trouble.

"Yeah, whatever," Denny says, "Later."

He heads off. I walk back home, carrying the guitar and my hat and thinking about Lisa and her cutlets. If you asked me, I'd say she doesn't *need* cutlets. But then, the day she'd ask me about something like that would be the day I became Santa Claus.

Chuck is in the basement again when I get home. I carry the guitar case downstairs. This time he's in his real-estate-guy clothes—dress pants and shoes, and a snappy leather jacket. He reels in a tape measure, then writes in a little notebook.

"Hey, Dave," he says. "Going to show a couple of houses. Need to measure up for drywall and hit the hardware store before I come back here to work. You around this aft? I might need a hand for a few minutes."

"Uh-huh," I say.

Chuck closes the notebook and nods at the guitar case. "Been busking?"

"We were shooting our video."

"Oh yeah. How'd it go?" Chuck reaches for the guitar case as he talks. I give it to him. After all, it is his guitar.

"It was okay." Why tell him about something no one's going to see? Chuck puts the case down and opens it. I remember the scratches on the guitar. Maybe now *would* be a good time to talk, to distract Chuck a little.

I say, "Denny filmed us busking, but it didn't work out. Then we went to the park and made stuff up, but I don't know if any of it is any good. We might have to do it again."

This is the most I've said all at once to a grown-up since I was ten. I'm not sure if it works or not.

Chuck is kneeling, looking at the guitar and running a hand over it. "Man," he says, "this baby's seen some hard traveling. I didn't realize I'd beaten it up that much, you know? Bar gigs will do that."

Part of me thinks *whew*, but now another part feels guilty. "Maybe busking does too," I say. "A little."

Chuck shrugs. "Hey, it never was the world's greatest. Long as it gets used." He digs a pick out of the case and plays a chugging little lick from a Chuck Berry song. "Still sounds good, huh?" He plays some more. "Man, am I rusty."

Chuck may be rusty, but he's good. He's a lot better than me, even if he does stick to geezer rock and country. I can tell from his chord positions that he's in the key of A. I take the bass from its open case, flip on the amp beside it and dial it down low. It's pretty easy to play along with Chuck. We get a little groove going.

"Nice," Chuck says. Then he blows the next part and laughs. He shakes his left hand. "My fingers hurt already!" He puts the guitar back in its case and closes it. Then he stands up, brushing off the knees of his pants. "I ever tell you about the video we tried for Razorburn?"

"No. One time you said you would." I turn off the amp and lean the bass against it.

Chuck laughs. "Okay, this was way back when videos were just getting big. We wanted to be out front, you know? So we decided to do a video for 'Look Slick,' one of our tunes. And naturally, we had to do the whole thing cheap. So we hired this guy—Stan, I think his name was—who said he could do it all. And we told Stan our ideas. Mainly they were about girls and convertibles, but the best part was that we'd video Gonzo, our drummer, getting his head shaved. Don't ask me why, but he was up for it. Drummers are crazy, you know?

"So Stan set up, and Gonzo's girl-friend, who was a babe, shaved his head while Stan filmed the whole thing. It went great. Gonzo had a major mullet to shave off, so hair was flying every-where. But underneath, it turned out he didn't look so slick. His head was all lumpy and pointy, and his ears stuck straight out. His girlfriend said they were like car doors. Man, it was grim.

"Gonzo was mad when he looked in a mirror, but we told him he'd taken a hit for the band. Stan told him it was great footage too. Now, you've gotta remember this was before digital cameras. So we gathered around for the playback, and that's when we found out one of the reasons Stan worked so cheap—he was the kind of guy who'd forget to load a tape in the camera."

Chuck laughs and shrugs to settle his leather jacket. "And that's what he'd done. There was nothing to see. I thought Gonzo was going to rip Stan apart right there. He was jumping up and down yelling, *I did this for nothing?* Like I said, drummers are crazy.

"Anyway, one look at Gonzo, and nobody else would get shaved. And we couldn't do it to him again, of course. His girlfriend said we could if we stuck a wig on him. I think they split up not long after that. Gonzo wore a Boston Bruins toque for the next three months, which was tough, 'cause it was summer. That was the end of our video."

Chuck starts to climb the stairs. I follow him, wondering if Stan and Denny could be related. Chuck heads off to the hardware store. I go online and find that Lisa is there too. I'm not sure what to message, except I know not to mention cutlets.

Finally I type, **Hi crazy day for sure. Think Denny can make it work?**

She messages back, **Think pigs have wings?**

Wings make me think of chickens, and chickens make me think of cutlets. Oh, no. Usually, talking with Lisa is easy, but now I have to choose every word carefully. I decide to type, **Busy 2nite? Want 2 do music or anything**

I'm hoping Lisa will pick up on the "anything." I'm about to send it when there's another message from Lisa. **Have 2 go now.**

## Chapter Nine

Denny sends the video Sunday afternoon. Usually my mom has an open house on Sundays, but today another agent is doing it for her. This is bad, because it means she's walking by when the video comes onscreen. I try to shut it down before she notices, but I'm too late.

"Is this it?" she cries. "Perfect! Let's see."

Now I've got no choice. The video is titled *Coming Apart at the Dreams*. The title turns out to be the last thing Denny's gotten right.

Everything else sucks. For the entire three minutes and twelve seconds. There are shots of us in the park and some of us busking. All of it is embarrassing. Lisa looks hot, but beside her I look like a toothpick in a straw hat and neck brace. The harmonica solo plays over shots of Doom Master posed in different places. Then, for a big finish, the colors go all overexposed and everything blurs. Oh, spare me.

It is every bad homemade band video you've ever seen rolled into one. The shots last forever. The camera jiggles every time Denny moves. The syncing is a mess. Our lips move when there's no singing and don't move when there is. Our guitar strums don't match the music.

The only plus side is that the video is so useless, we don't have to *decide* not to post it. It's a no-brainer that this should be deleted.

Not for Mom. "Heyyy," she says when it's finally over. "For a first try, I think it's…fun. That's what this is all about, right?"

No, that's not what this is all about. This is about me becoming rich and famous and so cool that girls—one especially—will chase me if I walk by. You can't explain that to your mom, though. You know?

So the answer I give her is, "Right."

"What was with the little robot toy?" she asks.

I'm not going there either. "We got a million dollars for a product placement," I say.

"All right, smart guy. Enough for now. Don't you have a history assignment due tomorrow?" Mom gives my shoulder a squeeze. "Anyway, I think you all did a great job."

There's a death sentence if I ever heard one.

Mom walks off. I click back through the screens to Denny's message. **Ready to post it. Sending you the blooper reel we put together hilarious lol.**

Yeah right. Denny has started using *we* as if he's a king or something. Maybe he has a history assignment too.

This reminds me that, for once, Mom is right. I should look at my homework. *Hilarious* can wait. I've had all I can take of video for one day. At least nobody is going to waste their time looking at this. I message him back. **Dream on. nothing to post. trash it B4 world sees u r not a genius.**

After that's taken care of, I do a little history homework. Not a *lot* of homework, so I'm kind of busy on Monday morning. I'm so busy, I don't even look for Lisa or Denny. It's only after I hand in my assignment that I get to breathe. That's when I get the feeling something is different.

I'm not sure exactly why I get the feeling. It's a bunch of little things. Like, why do those kids on the landing stop talking as I come down the stairs? What's with that whisper and laugh I hear behind me in the library? How come I feel eyes on me when I line up in the caf, but when I turn, it's as if everyone has just looked away? Why does a girl in English gasp as I walk into class? Why is there giggling when I get asked to read aloud? *What's going on?*

After English, I duck into a washroom and do a quick check. My fly is up, and my hair doesn't look any dorkier than usual. There are no new zit volcanoes on my face, and nobody has stuck a Kick Me sign to my back. My backpack is still pretty rank from the chocolate milk, but you have to be right up close to smell it. Is this all my imagination? Hey, I'm fourteen—I'm supposed to be self-conscious, right? I bet you are too.

But I go to math and my *teacher* is biting down on a grin as he asks me to do a problem. Nawww...he isn't. *Is he*? I mean, why would he be laughing at me?

This is weirding me out. After school, I don't stick around to find Denny and give him a hard time about the video. I want to go home, chill in the basement and let this feeling pass.

As I walk by the smokers on the corner, their voices drop. Am I going paranoid? I hustle home, give Arch some food and a scratch behind the ears, make a peanut-butter sandwich and head down to the almost-man cave.

Chuck got me to help him put some drywall up on Saturday afternoon, so you can't see into the man cave bathroom anymore. He says I can help him with the taping and mudding next, whatever those are. I flop into a beanbag chair, eat my sandwich and try not to think about it.

I decide the stuff at school was just my imagination. I'm reaching for the guitar case when I hear the front door. "Hi," Mom calls. I listen to the change in the sound of her footsteps as she walks from the tile at the front door, down the carpet in the hall and across the wooden kitchen floor. Then I watch her feet grow legs and a body as she thumps down the stairs.

"Hi, sweetie, how was your day?"

"Sensational as always, Mom."

"That's terrific." Sometimes my mom doesn't get sarcasm any more than Denny. "Got much homework?"

"Practically none," I lie.

"Lucky you. Then you can help Chuck. He texted that he'll be over after supper. I'm doing that chicken you like, so you're on table setting and salad."

"I didn't say I have *no* homework."

"Then come on up and do it before you set the table." Mom starts back up the stairs. All but her shins and feet have disappeared when she stops. "Say," she calls back down, "do you know a YouTube video called *Pop Top*?"

"Nope."

"Chuck's text said to check it out. Everyone at his office says it's a hoot."

"Gee, better jump right on that one." God knows what an office full of Chucks would call a hoot. I don't want to find out.

"Okay, smart guy. Up here for homework in five minutes." Mom goes upstairs. There are a few more footsteps, then nothing.

I pull out the guitar for a sec. Mom will remember the five minutes, but I can try to make them last.

I've just played the coolest chord I've ever heard, and I'm trying to figure out what it is when I hear the kitchen footsteps again. Mom's voice floats down. "Hey, get up here and check this out. Then you've got homework."

## Chapter Ten

I guess this is togetherness time. I head upstairs. Mom is at the kitchen table. She's sitting in front of her work laptop, holding Arch. The *Pop Top* video is cued up on the screen. The first image is a frozen orange blur.

"How long is it?" I ask. I don't know how much Chuck-style funny I can take.

Mom peers at the screen. "Three minutes and twelve seconds." Why does that time sound familiar? She pulls another chair out from the table. "Have a seat."

I sit on the edge of the chair. I'll give this thirty seconds, tops. Mom clicks on the Play icon.

Through the tiny speaker I hear an acoustic guitar strum. It's a rhythm and chord I know. A bass line kicks in. I know it too—I play it all the time. It's "Coming Apart at the Dreams." Hey, what is this?

The camera pulls back and into focus. The orange blur is the fuzzy lining of a guitar case, with Doom Master in the middle. I'm getting a very bad *oh-oh* feeling. But what *is* this? Did Denny go rogue? The shot switches to Lisa's tight pink top as she sways on the swings. The parts of her in that tight pink top bounce in slow-mo as you hear her sing,

*What's up? I'm down*
*When you're not around...*

And now, a flash close-up of my face with my eyes bulging out, as if I'm staring at her bouncing. I know it—it's from that day Denny surprised me with the camera.

*I could trip, I could fall*
*Would you hear if I called...*

Now I'm fast-motion stumbling into the guitar case and Lisa's jumping back, then my eyes bulge and I yell. Then there's a shot of Doom Master tumbled over on two white lumps—cutlets.

*I feel bad, I feel good*
*Like you knew that I would...*

Aw, *noooooo*...I can guess what's coming. Sure enough, there's Lisa doing the Heimlich on me, then a cutlet popping out of the neckline of her top and the harmonica popping out of my mouth. Cut to Doom Master on the ground, as if he's what I spat out.

*Over and over and over and over*
*Coming apart at the dreammmmmms...*

Over and over and over and over, there is Lisa's chest doing four stuttery fast-mo bounces on the teeter-totter, with a cutlet popping again and again and again and again. On *dreammmmms,* a cutlet sails through the air. Cut to Lisa turning away and fumbling with her top, then my bulging eyes again.

Can it get worse? Of course it does. The first verse repeats, and this time you see my butt-first crash landing on the teeter-totter. It's a horror show. I'm frozen, my eyes locked on the screen for all three minutes and twelve seconds, including the last bit, where a flying cutlet takes out Doom Master. Every second makes us look like idiots. As an added bonus, I look like a pervert, too.

It doesn't help that I hear Mom snorting, giggling, then just plain laughing beside me. When it's over, I can't look at her. I may never look at anyone again. In fact, I may never come out of the man cave again.

Mom wipes her eyes and says, "That's—how did—did you plan it all first, or make it up as you went along?"

"It just happened," is all I can answer. Then I add, "Somehow."

"Well, you're naturals, then."

Right, I think. Natural disasters. Is Denny suddenly on drugs or something? Where did this come from? What happened?

Mom scoots Arch off her lap and stands up. I stand up too. As I do, I notice my fingernails have dug into the table. Mom hasn't even noticed anything's wrong.

"You and Lisa were such good sports to let yourselves look silly," she says. "How did you dream all that up?"

"It's hard to say." I'm going to find out though. Behind me, Mom opens the fridge. I start for the man cave. I need a moment to myself before I begin finding out.

"No one will see it," I say to myself. I'm at the top of the stairs.

I guess I say it out loud, because Mom says, "Oh sure they will! Don't worry about that, hon. There have been a ton of views already. Look at the number."

I don't want to go back and look at the number. I might throw up if I look at the number. "Just tell me if it's over seven hundred," I say. That would be almost half my high school. That might also explain the weird stuff this afternoon.

I hear Mom walk over to check the screen. "Let's see…way more than that." She laughs. "It's almost six figures."

"What does that mean?"

"Nearly a hundred thousand."

I almost fall down the stairs.

Mom comes over and smiles. "See? I told you. You're a hit!"

A hit. I feel as if I've *been* hit, with a sledgehammer. "Sure," I say. "Right." My voice sounds as if I'm choking.

Mom gives my shoulder a squeeze. "Aww, hon," she says. "Having second thoughts? Don't be embarrassed. It's fun. You went for it! All these hits mean people *like* it." The squeeze turns into a hug. I have to say I need one just now. And then the sledgehammer hits me again. What about Lisa? Has she seen this? I have to warn her. What if she's seen it and thinks I did it? Will she

73

even listen? What am I going to say? As I stumble back downstairs, all I know for sure is, I'm going to get Denny for this if it's the last thing I ever do.

# Chapter Eleven

Lisa doesn't answer her phone. She doesn't answer my texts. She's not online. Maybe she's sick or too busy with homework to answer or go online and see the video.

Yeah right, and maybe I'm Doom Master.

Denny doesn't answer his phone. He doesn't answer my texts. He's not online.

*He's* not sick or busy with homework. He's...never mind. I'm not going to say what Denny is.

I help Chuck with the drywall, which is not bad, because he only mentions the video once. "That's the kind of thing Gonzo would have done after a few brewskis," Chuck says. I think it's a compliment.

The next morning Mom's already dressed for work when I come into the kitchen. She's finishing her coffee. Her laptop is open on the table again. "Hey, video star," she says, "Guess what? Nine hundred and thirty-eight thousand and twelve—no, fifteen hits. You've gone viral!"

I wonder if I can say I'm sick and then hide in the man cave all day. I know it's not going to happen. Besides, I want to find Denny and yell at him.

I keep my earbuds in and the hood of my hoodie up all the way to school.

It's no use. Before I get to my locker, I get asked six times to do the bulging eyes and three times to "fall over like that." A teacher tells me we are featured on *badmusicvideos.com*.

"Thanks," I say, and I wish I could climb inside my locker and stay there till suppertime.

I can't. I have to go to class. All morning I feel people looking at me, especially every time I want to do a quick nose dig or pick at a zit. All morning I hear the whispers and giggles. By lunch I'm way tired of being asked if I have a Doom Master sandwich today. And there's still no Lisa and no Denny. Denny and I have gym together last period. He'd better be there.

I make sure to get to the change room almost too late for class. That way most of the guys are already out in the gym. A couple are left though.

"Hey, Pop Top!"

"Do the eyes!"

"No, fall on your butt!"

It turns out that I have a secret weapon against them when I open my backpack.

"Whoa, baby!"

"Something die in there, Ace?"

They hustle out. I pull on my shorts and T-shirt. By now they smell so disgusting, they're grossing even me out. Maybe I'll feed them to Denny after I finish yelling at him. I head into the gym. And there's Denny. I start toward him. The gym teacher's whistle blows. "All right, three gym laps to warm up, then pair up on the mats with your wrestling partner."

Guess who my partner is going to be? Denny doesn't look at me, but he must know I'm after him, because he runs way faster than usual. We're both out of breath by the time the whistle blows.

"Oh, hi, Ace,'" he pants, as if he's just noticed me. Then, "Wow, man, no offense, but it might be time to wash your gym stuff."

"Yeah, well, you'd know all about stinking a place out, Den. What did you think you were do—"

"Denny, Ace, put a lid on it," calls the gym teacher. Then he calls me out onto the mat so he can demonstrate a new takedown. I get down on my knees in defense position, and the teacher fake-gasps.

"Something die and you roll in it, Ace? Time to do a little laundry, huh?" he says. Everyone laughs but me. Then he grabs me like I'm a couple of dry twigs and tells the class, "Now, if I do this takedown right, Ace's eyes are going to bulge out like they did on his video." There's another laugh, then he squashes me.

When I get back to Denny, I try squashing him. I'm not very good at it, but it must hurt a little, because after the third time, Denny says, with his face in the mat, "Okay, okay, take it easy."

"Why should I?" I get off him. "You made us look like goofs."

"Oh, come on. It's just stuff from the blooper reel. I told you I made one."

"That's no blooper reel, Den. It was all put together and synced with the music."

"No, but it was stuff from the blooper reel. We only put it together for fun. And I didn't post it."

"We? Who's we? Who posted it?"

"The girls, I guess. Hey, it's your turn to get down."

I kneel on the gym mat. "What girls?"

Denny gets down beside me. "You know. Nadia and Alison, from video club. They helped me with some of the editing for the real video. After, we were goofing around with some of the other bits, and we shot a little bit more. It was pretty funny when Alison threw the cutlets in the air. I never would have guessed Lisa used cutlets, would you? I mean, if they were hers."

*"Nadia and Alison helped you?"*

"Yeah, why? It's no biggie." Denny grabs my arms and dumps me to the mat.

"They both hate Lisa, you dork."

"They do? Why?"

"I don't know," I say. It's hard to breathe with Denny on top of me. "Get off." I get back on my knees. "It's something about boys is all I know. So take the stupid video down."

"I can't." Denny grabs me again. "Anyway, it's already gone viral. Besides, this isn't just about you, Ace. Think about me. I've got my fans, my career. This is huge for me. I can't take down my first big hit."

*"Fans? Career? What fa—"*

Denny dumps me to the mat. "Hey, Ace, I know girls. Nobody meant anything bad by it. It's like a *collage*. It's supposed to be *ironic*. It's part of my *oeuvre*."

"Your what?" I say into the mat. "You don't even know what those words mean." Neither do I. I'll have to look them up. "Get *off* me!"

Denny lets me up. I look at him. "Sorry." He shrugs.

The thing is, he's telling the truth. I've known Denny since grade two. He's not a good liar. I glare at him. Denny says, "Look on the bright side. You wanted your music out there, right?"

## Chapter Twelve

Denny is right. We did want our music out there. But it's not the music everyone is paying attention to, is it? No, it's the bulging eyes and flying cutlets.

I walk home after school. I'm pretty sure a couple of random people on the street stare at me. It's a spooky feeling, knowing a million people have watched you acting like a goof. Is this what being famous is all about? If it is, I think it's kind of sick.

And is this how girls fight with each other? If it is, I think that's kind of sick too.

By now I've texted Lisa about a thousand times. There's never an answer. I do the only thing I can think of. When Mom gets home, I ask her to drive me to Bargain Village after dinner. Lisa usually works Tuesday nights.

Mom says sure. As she answers a couple of emails at the kitchen table, I see the tag *badmusicvideos.com* in the text on her laptop screen. Mom knows. She doesn't talk about the video once, which is pretty cool of her. When we get to Bargain Village, Mom waits in the car. I think she also knows I need to talk to Lisa, even though I don't tell her.

The store is way too bright and way too crammed with stuff. The hum from the lights mixes with a lame classic rock station on the sound system. A big lady wearing a red vest stares at me from the cashier desk as if I'm a shoplifter.

It takes me a couple of minutes to find Lisa. The big lady gives me the hairy eyeball the whole time. Bargain Village is not exactly hopping with shoppers right now.

Lisa is stocking shelves near the back. She's wearing a red vest too. As soon as she sees me, she turns her back. "Get lost."

"But—" I begin, and before I can say anything else, she spins around. She's got bags of tube socks in each hand. "My whole life is wrecked," she hisses. "How did you ever get me to do this?"

"But—"

"I'm a joke, the music is a joke, everything is a joke, except it isn't funny. Or maybe you think it is. You and Denny." She spits Denny's name out as if it's a moldy potato chip.

"*No, no!* Not even Denny thinks so. And he didn't do it. Alison and—"

"I know they did it! They sent me the link. But idiot Denny helped them."

"He didn't know what they were doing. He thought it was, um, ironic, like a collage or something." While I say this, I'm asking myself, *Why am I sticking up for Denny?*

"*Ironic?* A *collage?*" Lisa rams the socks into a bin, then rips open a cardboard box. It's full of packs of boxer shorts. "Don't you get what this is all about? Alison and all of them hate me, so they made me look stupid in front of a million people. Don't you know anything about girls?" She scoops out an armload of boxer shorts and almost throws them onto a shelf. Some fall on the floor.

I pick them up. "Why do they hate you?"

"Because Alison thinks I stole Rob."

"Who's Rob?"

"My *boyfriend*. Sorry, make that *ex*-boyfriend. He broke up with me by text and Facebook because he says he feels humiliated. *He* feels humiliated. Do you know what it feels like to have your boyfriend break up with you by text and then go online with it after a million people have watched you pop your cutlets in a video?"

All I can say is, "Uh, probably not."

All I can think is, Boyfriend? *Boyfriend*? I stand there with the boxer shorts in my hands. I'm too stunned to do anything with them.

"No kidding." Lisa is crying now. She grabs the boxers from me and throws them at the shelf. Most of them fall back on the floor. I say, "I didn't, uh, know you had…"

"Why would you? He's away at private school. We all met him last year when he went to our school, before you came. Rob never liked you and me doing music together, and now he's dumped me. *Online.*"

Her shoulders are shaking, she's crying so hard, and she's got her hands over her face.

I still don't know what to do. I pick up the boxers, to not look totally useless. "Oh, just leave them," she sobs. I keep holding them anyway, because it seems even dumber to drop them again.

"Well," I say before I even think about it, "he's an idiot if he dumped you." This does not seem to help. Lisa keeps right on crying, her hands still over her face. My own face feels all hot. I put the boxers on the shelf. A couple of packs fall right off again. "Sorry," I say. I back away. Lisa is still crying.

The big lady is still giving me the evil eye as I walk to the door. As I pass the cash, she breaks into this big smile. "I thought it was you," she says. "That video you did with Lisa was *so* funny."

# Chapter Thirteen

Mom drives us home. Chuck's suv is out front. As we go inside, I hear a toilet flush in the basement. It's the soundtrack for my life.

I help Chuck for a while. He has me put primer paint on the bathroom walls while he does more mudding and taping on the other side. Chuck doesn't say anything about the video either.

Maybe Mom talked to him. I'm starting to wonder which is worse, people who bug me about it or people who know but don't say a word. When they don't say anything, I worry about what they're thinking.

"Place is shaping up," Chuck says on the other side of the wall. Until I saw this one get built, I never knew how little there is to a wall. I always thought they were solid stone or wood or something.

"Uh-huh," I say.

"Think you're gonna like it?"

"Uh-huh." Truthfully, I don't know, and right now I don't care. I kind of liked the place the way it was, when it was too grungy for adults to want to come down here.

"Good," Chuck says. "And you know, if your mom ever decides to sell the place, it'll raise the value."

"Why would she do that?" I say. I don't even care. I hear Chuck clear his throat.

"Oh. Well, ah, I don't know. Just saying. But either way, you have a cool place to hang out."

I roll on more primer paint. I guess so. It doesn't feel like my place though. Maybe that doesn't matter. I mean, what am I going to do here anyway? My music career is over. The way Lisa's feeling, I'm guessing Two is down to one, so there's no need to practice here. And Denny's not rushing over to hang out either. I'm getting a man cave exactly when I don't need one. Oh man, I wish I could go busking with Lisa again, even if I played the harmonica upside down and looked dumb every time.

I finish painting and tell Chuck I have to go do some homework. I go upstairs and lie on my bed. I stare at the ceiling. Then I get up and really do some homework. Don't ask me why. To keep from thinking about other stuff, I guess.

When I get to school the next morning, it's more of the same. I'm at my locker when someone yells, "Ace! Catch!" and what looks like a cutlet comes flying at me.

In homeroom, someone says "Doom Master" in this deep voice and then rips a big belch. In first period, biology class, the teacher says something about a Heimlich maneuver and digestion, and the whole class breaks up. Except for me.

By period two, I'm feeling totally alone. Denny is off being Denny somewhere. After last night, I'm not even going to look for Lisa. I'm walking to class when I feel my phone vibrate. It's a message from Lisa: **mus rm@ lunch k?**

My insides do a nosedive. If you thought I was feeling bad before, try me now. I feel as if I'm about to do a face-plant from fifty stories. This is it. I know it. This is when she's going to tell me officially what I already know. Two is over. I've totally blown it. Oh man, why did I go and see her last night? Why did I have to make it worse? Why did I ever listen to Denny?

I drag myself through period two, and then I make myself walk to the music room. I don't think I've ever walked to the music room slowly before. The longer I take, the longer Lisa and I are still playing music together.

I hear voices before I even get to the door. One of them is Lisa's. "It'll be so great," she is saying, "…perfect timing… change everything!" She sounds *happy* it's over. Oh, no.

"Excellent," says another voice. "That'll be so cool." It's a guy's voice.

"So tell everybody, okay?"

"Hey, for sure." I know this voice. It's a grade-eleven guy who's a good bass player. I look in. Sure enough, he's there, along with another guy who plays drums. It's worse than I thought. Lisa has already started her next band. I'm backing away as she turns around. "Ace! Anyway, later," she says to the guys.

*Yeah*, I think, *you can talk more about your new band after I'm gone.* I start backing out again.

Lisa runs over. "Where are you going? You just got here. Listen, I have to tell you something." Now she's all serious and intense.

"Sure." My knees have turned to mashed potatoes. This must be a world record. I'm being dumped by a girl without ever having had her for my girlfriend.

She flips her hair back the way she does and bites her lip. Then she says quickly, "Listen, um, sorry about last night. I just lost it, you know? With everything?" Her face is pink.

"That's okay." I'm thinking, *Let's get to the "you're history" part.* That way

I'll have time to eat lunch, throw it all up, get teased some more and still be in time to get beaten up in gym. Now that it's happening to me, I don't see why face-to-face is supposed to be so great for getting dumped. A quick text would make it easier for me to crawl away and die.

But Lisa isn't ready yet. She says, "Anyway, this morning I felt so rotten that I was going to ditch again, but then I got this message—"

"And Rob your boyfriend said he was sorry," I blurt, sounding sarcastic. *And you promised him you wouldn't do music with me anymore.* At least I stop myself from saying that part.

"What?" She tucks in her chin and gives me a look. "He's never said he's sorry in his life. Anyway, he doesn't have anything to do with this." She waves her hand. Her words are spilling on the floor, she's talking so fast now.

"So, like I said, I got this message. It was a forward from Denny, and it was from this woman who's a producer for *Garden Avenue Kids*."

"Huh?"

"You know, the TV show."

"Oh, yeah." I do know. It's a pretty good show, for one that doesn't have galactic death rays. It's about some kids at a school like ours.

Lisa is racing on, her voice getting higher. "And she saw the video and found out how to contact Denny in his channel details and asked him to send us a message that *she liked the song! And she wants to pay us to use it on one of the episodes because it sounds like something two of the characters might record!* Isn't that fantastic? We *did* it!" Lisa grabs my arms and shakes me. "We did it, we did it!" She is jumping up and down. I think I am too. First, though, I have to ask.

"Are you sure it's for real? This *is* from Denny, right?"

"It is, it is! There was an email address in the message, and I emailed her right away and she got back to me. It's the real thing. We've got to text the whole world," Lisa says, "and then we've got to celebrate. What should we do?"

There are lots of answers for that, but for once I know the best one. "Let's play some music."

## Chapter Fourteen

I can hardly wait. We meet at the liquor
store after school. I open Chuck's guitar
case and prop up our cardboard sign
that reads *Broken String Fund.* We sling
on our guitars, I pull my harp rack on,
and we tune up.

"Ready?"

"Ready."

We're barely done the first song when someone tosses money in the case and says, "Are you the ones on YouTube?"

"Yup," I say.

"Will you do that song?"

"Sure." Lisa smiles. We play "Coming Apart at the Dreams" the best we ever have. I even get the harmonica part just right. By the end, there's a small crowd. They clap.

Then someone says to Lisa, "How come you didn't, you know, pop your…" Someone else calls to me, "Hey, aren't you gonna fall into the guitar case and do the eyes?"

Lisa turns away as if she doesn't hear. I say, "Can't today. Doctor's orders. It's an insurance thing." I don't know what I'm talking about, but it seems to work. "Listen for our song on *Garden Avenue Kids*," I call, and I start to strum.

Lisa picks up on it. "Here's a Neil Young song."

Lisa sings it great, but people drift away. Stuff like that happens twice more in the next half hour. I know that's how busking works, but still. Are the dumb bits all anybody wants from us? Lisa doesn't look any happier.

I say, "Remember at lunch today, when you said *we did it*?"

"Sure. Why?"

"Um, maybe it's not *we*. Maybe it's Denny, Nadia and Alison. *We* didn't make us go viral."

Lisa shakes her head. "No way. They didn't do that *for* us, they did it *to* us. We wrote the song. We win. That's what's important. It serves them right."

I'm about to say it doesn't feel as if we're winning right now when a guy walks up and says, "Hey, are you the—"

"Yup," I say.

"Will you do the song?" He holds up a twenty. Maybe Lisa's right after all.

Lisa says, "With all the comedy stuff?"

"Well, yeah." The guy shrugs as if it's a no-brainer.

Lisa looks at me. I look at her. What now? Twenty bucks is twenty bucks. Is it worth acting dumb for?

Lisa smiles at the guy. "We'll do the song, but we can't do the comedy today. Ace hurt his neck doing the video, and his doctor won't let him. Sorry."

We start to play. The guy pockets his twenty and tosses in a five instead. "Thanks," he says halfway through and walks off.

We finish and look at each other again. "Hey," I say, "a five is still great."

Lisa nods. "But…" Then she shakes her head and sighs. "I see what you mean."

I check my tuning while I try to find something to say. "Hey," I remind us both, "the producer for *Garden Avenue Kids* doesn't want the comedy. She wants the song." I check my sixth string. It's flat. "Maybe when people hear it there, they'll pay more attention."

"Yeah," Lisa says, "you're right." I tune up my sixth string, and then she says, "Would you do it again?"

"What? Like, the video?"

"Yeah. But on purpose. Would you act stupid to get attention?"

"Well," I say, "Denny does it all the time."

Lisa rolls her eyes. "No, but say it was to get attention for another song? I guess I mean, was this worth it?" She sighs, and her shoulders slump. "Like, it *did* work out. But think about the last couple of days. Even busking was more fun before everyone wanted us to act silly. If that's what you have to do to get people to listen, it's pretty lame. In fact, it's horrible." Now Lisa plucks a string and checks her tuner. She looks down, then at me. She's waiting for an answer.

I say, "I don't know. Maybe it would be okay if I thought people were laughing with me, not at me."

"How would you know for sure?"

*That's* a tough question. I shrug.

Lisa says, "I don't know either. Maybe you couldn't know. But what do you think? Would you do it?"

Answers crowd my head. One of them is *Nooooo.* One of them is *For a million dollars.* The one that comes out is, "Maybe…with you." The "with you" kind of trails off into a mumble though.

Lisa smiles and does some more tuning. "One more," she says. "Then I have to go. What should we do?"

"'I'm A Believer.' We haven't done that yet."

It's an easy one, and people like it because they know it from *Shrek*. Lisa even does the accent the second time through, and I have a harmonica bit. When I open my eyes after my solo, guess who's standing in front of me?

As the song ends, Denny says, "Yo, don't thank me, just throw money my way." He's looking in the guitar case as he says it.

"How about bricks?" I say.

Denny doesn't get it, as usual. His arms flap around. "I told you it would work! I told you a video would get your song out there! And now a million people know my name and style."

"And think that Lisa and I are nimrods. You left out that part, Den."

"C'mon, Ace. You win some, you lose some. Just be glad I check all the comments on my YouTube account. Do you think you could show that producer some of my other stuff?"

Lisa doesn't say anything. She puts her own guitar away. Now she scoops the money from my guitar case and puts it on top of hers. She kneels down to divide it up. I take down our sign and put Chuck's guitar away. I remove the harp rack and tuck my pick in my pocket. "What other stuff?" I finally say to Denny.

"Well, there's the Doom Master footage from your place to work with, but what I'm really thinking is, we all do a follow-up. I've got this great idea. We need to make fake space suits and get helmets. Have you got a song that would go with that?"

"Not yet," I say. "All the rest of our songs are about zombies, but we'll get right on it."

"Yessss," Denny says. "Zombies in space!"

I don't even try to answer. Lisa stands up. "In your dreams, Denny."

She hands me my money. It looks like quite a bit. I stuff it in my pocket to count later.

"I've got to go," she says to me, "or I won't get to work on time." To Denny she says, "Thanks for sending the message, Denny. Don't thank your gal pals for us, 'kay? Later."

Lisa grabs her guitar case and heads off down the street. Denny calls, "Will do, Lee. *Ciao!*" Then he says to me, "Hey, want to see a movie Friday? *Death Watch III* is opening. My dad can drive."

"Yeah, why n—" I start to say. Then I say, "Wait. Watch my guitar." All at once, I know I have two questions to ask, and they're not for Denny. One is for when I get home. I have to ask Mom if she is thinking of selling the house. The other I can ask right now. I run down the street. "Lisa! Lee!"

She turns. I catch up to her. We're face-to-face. It's now or never. I pant, "Uh, ah, on, um, Friday, do you, uh, maybe want to do, like, a movie or something?"

Ted Staunton divides his time between writing and a busy schedule as a speaker, workshop leader, storyteller and musical performer for children and adults. When he's not writing or presenting, Ted likes to perform with the Maple Leaf Champions Jug Band. He also enjoys running, reading and listening to music. Ted and his family live in Port Hope, Ontario. For more information, visit www.tedstauntonbooks.com.